THIS WALKER BOOK BELONGS TO:

For Annie, Sophia, Laurie, Solomon
and all the children of the city
K. H.

For my mum and dad
P. H.

First published 1996 by Walker Books Ltd
87 Vauxhall Walk, London SE11 5HJ

This edition published 1998

4 6 8 10 9 7 5

Text © 1996 Kathy Henderson
Illustrations © 1996 Paul Howard

This book has been typeset in Stempel Schneidler.

Printed in Hong Kong/China

British Library Cataloguing in Publication Data
A catalogue record for this book is
available from the British Library.

ISBN 0-7445-6042-X

THE YEAR IN THE CITY

Written by **Kathy Henderson**

Illustrated by **Paul Howard**

WALKER BOOKS
AND SUBSIDIARIES
LONDON • BOSTON • SYDNEY

The year's turning, the year's turning

through the streets
and the houses
where the people pass
and the traffic churns,
all the time
the year keeps turning.

JANUARY starts.

It's dark in the morning
and the trees are as bare
as the TV aerials.

Everyone's setting
off for work.
There are the children
kicking round the bus-stop.
The drivers scrape ice
off their frozen cars.

Nobody talks.
They breathe out steam,
hurry along
past the cold street birds
and down the stairs
into the underground.

Rush.
Squash.

Squeeze.
Push.

Rattling warm
into the centre
of town.

Hey look!
It's snowing!
Fat flakes floating
out of the sky,
trying to turn the city white.
    Some hope!
        Here come the children
        for a snowball fight.
The shopkeepers grumble
and get out their shovels.
And the drivers?
    They just carry on.
    Wheels spin.
        Skid.
                        Slide.

"Watch
    that car!"   CRASH!

There's a helicopter
chattering in the sky
watching all the traffic.
Nee-naw, nee-naw.
And more:
there are the first snowdrops.

FEBRUARY clatters.
Tin cans rattle.
A bitter wind lashes at the
rubbish in the gutter.
Sirens wail
and monsters roar.
Nee-naw, nee-naw.
There's a police car flashing by.
An ambulance races
close behind.

Through the crowds by the
restaurants in Chinatown
a paper lion leaps and sways
dancing the Chinese
New Year in.

The children laugh
and stare and cling.
And all the time
the cold wind sings.
Here comes spring.

MARCH stretches.

The days grow.
It's time to wash
the windows,
clean the house.

Look up there!
The tree men are cutting back
the big plane trees
before the leaves come out.
They've got chainsaws roaring,
gnawing at the branches
till they fall into a tangle
on the road below.

And the street sweeper's out,
there's a lorry cleaning drains,
the washing lines are flapping
but here comes more rain.
A woman cleans windscreens
when the traffic lights go red
and even the buses at the depot
take their turn
in the giant rollers
of the big bus-wash.

APRIL's bursting.
The supermarket's packed
with chocolate eggs
and fluffy chicks
and food for Passover
and queues.
The bill-sticker slaps
a clean advertisement
over the torn one on the hoarding.
"It's fresh! It's new!
It's SPRING!" it says.
"ANY-OLD-IRON?"
the scrap man's calling.

At the city farm
by the railway tracks
there are newborn piglets,
lambs, a calf.
And it's the Easter holidays,
there are children and babies
all over the place.

The sparrows up
in the broken gutter
line their nests
with old sweet wrappers.

Everything comes out in MAY,
the trees,
the cyclists,
the ice-cream signs.
It's time to go
to the park and play.
The nursery children
skip around throwing blossom
at each other.
"Look at that jogger!"
"Funny shorts!"

"Can we feed the ducks?"
"Ooh, there's baby ones!"
At the café
by the tennis courts
the old people chat,
pigeons fight for crumbs.
There's a wedding
on the town hall steps.
"Smile please!"
CLICK.
"Thank you."

Next thing
you know,
summer's here.

JUNE blooms.

The nights are short.
The air is full of grassy smells.
Very early in the morning
at the wholesale market
huge lorries drive in
from the countryside.

They're full of vegetables,
fruit and flowers
picked from the fields
only hours ago.
Those yawning
shopkeepers come to buy
goods to fill their shops
for opening time
and drive off through
the just-waking city.
Along the streets
the roses bloom,
hedges are clipped
and mowers drone
and strange things grow
in the strangest places.

JULY sweats,
windows wide open.
Just listen to the city
roaring in the heat!
At lunchtime
the office workers pour
into the squares
to find some air.
The big trees rustle.
The traffic fumes.

A masked man with a spray
walks by
killing the weeds
between the paving stones.
And here's the
Junior School Summer Fair!
There's a steel band and
a fancy-dress parade.
There's Grandpa
dozing in the shade
next to fifty children
jumping up and down,
squealing and laughing
on a bouncy castle
'cos school has only
a few days left to run.

Then
AUGUST sighs.

Trainloads of people
leave the stations.
Cars piled high
with tents and cases,
welly boots and suntan cream
are setting off for the motorways,
getting away for the holidays,
leaving the streets
to their August ways ...

and to the tourists
who come in high-top buses
with their cameras and sunglasses.
They go for boat trips
on the river,
troop in and out
of museums and churches
and into the squares
to stand and stare
at dozy dogs on dusty doorsteps,
tired winds swirling the litter,
children flopping
in the sprinklers
trying to get cool.

August days are lazy days
and even the traffic's
half asleep.

Autumn's here!
SEPTEMBER snaps.
The roads hum.
Wake up! Time for work!
The children set off
back to school
with heavy bags
and stiff
new shoes.

The little ones
are clinging
to their parents' hands
all terror and excitement
on their first day
at school.

On Saturday
down at the football ground
the season starts
and the big match brings
a crowd that sways
and chants and sings,
while out in the park
the first
leaves
fall.

OCTOBER pauses.

Golden. Still.
But there's so much work
to be done before winter.
There's the painter
hurrying to finish
the drainpipes
and the windowsills.

The roofers bang the last nails in
and take down their
scaffolding poles.

The children squabble for conkers.
Ice-cream vans play hopeful tunes
but the sweet shop man
cleans out his freezer,
"No more now
till next summer comes."
And down at the allotments
there are potatoes and carrots
to dig up and store.

The days are shrinking,
the nights are growing
and children dressed-up
as witches and ghosts
haunt the pavements
calling, "Trick or treat?"

Then overnight
NOVEMBER strikes.

Now a cold wind
whips the branches,
strips the last leaves off the trees
and chases them along the streets.
They block the drains.
Then it rains.
Big puddles grow
and passing traffic
throws up waves
of water at the forest of
umbrellas walking by.

At the doctors' surgery
the waiting room's full
of sniffing and coughing,
aching heads and babies crying.
"Next please."

The doctors see them
one by one
but there are always
more to come
and the dark days get
still darker.

Winter's back.

Then the
lights
go on.
DECEMBER glitters.

Shoppers crowd the pavements
by the big city stores
searching for gifts.
See the Christmas trees?
Where the warm air comes up
from the underground

there's a woman in a heap
wrapped in
old coats and string.
She's got holes in her shoes.
She's got nowhere to sleep.
The carol singers
clink their tins and sing
and the crowds hustle by
in their smart winter clothes
on their way to a show,
going out, hurrying home.
They'll be cosy indoors
while the dark days pass.
The shops shut.
Christmas comes at last.

And when it's all over
and the table's cleared,
late on the last
night of December,
the wide-awake city
waits to hear
the clock
strike
midnight   because…

The year's turning,
the year's turning.
See the people dance
and kiss and sing?
Hear the bells ring
and the cars hoot?
Here's January again.

The years keep turning.

MORE WALKER PAPERBACKS
For You to Enjoy

THE LITTLE BOAT
by Kathy Henderson/Patrick Benson

Winner of the Kurt Maschler Award

This is the story of a little polystyrene boat's voyage across the ocean –
its many adventures and encounters – until it comes to land once more.

"Captivating… What makes this story particularly special is the magical combination of the poetry
of the text and the delicacy of the illustrations. It will be enjoyed by a wider age range
than the average picture book." *The Good Book Guide*

0-7445-5253-2   £4.99

IN THE MIDDLE OF THE NIGHT
by Kathy Henderson/Jennifer Eachus

While one world sleeps, another comes to life – the world of nightworkers
in the city: nurses, bakers, cleaners, mail-sorters…

"A great picture book, lovely." *Chris Powling, BBC Radio*

0-7445-3143-8   £4.99

JOHN JOE AND THE BIG HEN
by Martin Waddell/Paul Howard

No one wants to mind little John Joe, which is why he's all alone in the
Brennans' yard one sunny afternoon, faced by the Brennans' big hen!

"The simplest of stories by a master of the picture-book text…
The perfect bedtime book for the very young." *Books for Keeps*

0-7445-5243-5   £4.99

Walker Paperbacks are available from most booksellers, or by post from B.B.C.S., P.O. Box 941, Hull, North Humberside HU1 3YQ

24 hour telephone credit card line 01482 224626

To order, send: Title, author, ISBN number and price for each book ordered, your full name and address, cheque or postal order payable to BBCS for the total amount and allow the following for postage and packing:
UK and BFPO: £1.00 for the first book, and 50p for each additional book to a maximum of £3.50.
Overseas and Eire: £2.00 for the first book, £1.00 for the second and 50p for each additional book.

Prices and availability are subject to change without notice.